My Classic Stories

Rapunzel

This book belongs to

Age   -----------

*Enjoy this book,
love from*   Rapunzel

This edition first published in 2013 by Ginger Fox Ltd
Copyright © 2013 Ginger Fox Ltd

Published in the UK by:
Ginger Fox Ltd
Stirling House, College Road
Cheltenham GL53 7HY
United Kingdom

www.gingerfox.co.uk

Retold by Nina Filipek
Illustrated by Katherine Kirkland

ISBN: 978-1-909290-00-6

10 9 8 7 6 5 4 3 2 1

Printed and bound in China.

Rapunzel

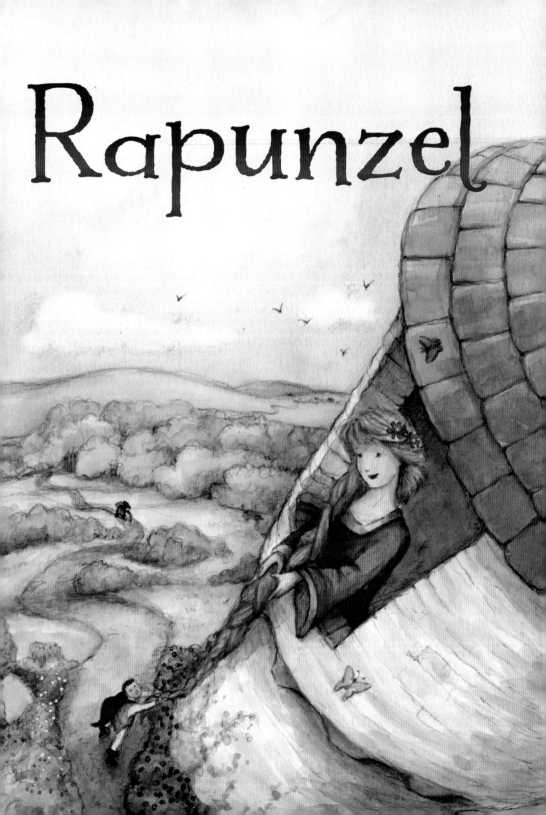

Once upon a time a husband and wife lived next door to a beautiful garden.

One day the wife longed to taste the radishes that grew there.

But there was one problem – the garden belonged to a wicked witch.

The husband thought the **wicked witch** would not notice if he took a few radishes.

7

He was very wrong! The wicked witch caught him in her garden. "How dare you steal my radishes!" she shouted.

The man explained how his wife longed
to taste them.

"You can take as many as you like,"
said the wicked witch,
"if you **promise** to give
me your **first baby!**"
The man was so afraid
that he agreed.

A year later, a baby girl
was born to the man and his wife.

And on that very same day the
wicked witch came and took the baby away.

The baby was called Rapunzel.

When Rapunzel grew up, the **wicked witch** locked her in a tower in the forest.

The tower had no stairs, no door and just one window at the top.

12

The wicked witch visited every day, calling out,

"Rapunzel!
Rapunzel!
Let down your hair!"

Rapunzel's hair had grown very long while
she had been imprisoned in the tower,
and the wicked witch would climb up her
beautiful golden plait as if it were a rope.

One day, a handsome prince was riding in the forest when he heard Rapunzel singing.

He also heard the wicked witch, and saw her climb up the tower, and he was curious.

After the wicked witch had gone, he called out,

"Rapunzel!
Rapunzel!
Let down your hair!"

Rapunzel was very surprised to see the prince instead of the wicked witch!

Every day after this, the prince visited
Rapunzel in the tower.

But one day the **wicked witch** saw him.
She was furious but she waited for him to
leave. Then she climbed up the tower and
cut off Rapunzel's beautiful golden hair!

The **wicked witch** snatched
Rapunzel from the tower
and left her in a great desert.

17

The next day the prince called out,

"Rapunzel!
Rapunzel!
Let down your hair!"

So the wicked witch held Rapunzel's plait out of the window and the prince started to climb.

When the prince reached the top of the tower and saw the wicked witch, he fell back in horror!

Thorns at the bottom of the tower blinded the prince.

"Now you will never see her again!"

laughed the wicked witch.

For months, the prince searched for Rapunzel.

By chance, at last, he reached the great desert where she lived.

Although he could not see Rapunzel, he heard her singing.

When Rapunzel saw him she cried with joy and her tears fell into the prince's eyes.

And then a wonderful thing happened ...

Her tears cleared the darkness away from the prince's eyes, and he was suddenly able to see again!

Together they escaped from the desert, and returned to the prince's castle, where the **wicked witch** never bothered them again.

Rapunzel and the prince got married,
and lived happily ever after.

Can you remember?

Now that you have read the story,
try to answer these questions about it.

1. What grew in the
   wicked witch's garden?

2. Why was the **wicked witch**
   angry with the husband?

?

3. What did the husband promise?

4. What did the **wicked witch**
   call out to Rapunzel?

5. Where did the **wicked witch**
   lock Rapunzel? Was it:

In a tower?
OR
In a castle?

Did you spot?

The wicked witch spotted the prince going to Rapunzel, but did you see who else was watching? See if you can find them all.

1. Did you see the rabbits hiding in the wicked witch's vegetable garden?

2. Which three little animals were keeping Rapunzel company in the tower?

3. What colour were the thorn bush's flowers?

4. Who was sitting on a rock watching, when Rapunzel and the prince were in the desert?

5. Who do you think the two elderly people were who were celebrating Rapunzel's marriage?

True or false?

Can you answer these true or false
questions correctly?

1. Radishes grew in the **wicked witch**'s garden.
True or false?

2. Rapunzel had very short hair.
True or false?

3. The **wicked witch** could climb
up Rapunzel's plait.
True or false?

4. The prince found Rapunzel
living in the jungle.
True or false?

5. "I helped the
prince to see again."
True or false?

Such a puzzle ...

Look carefully at the pictures below
and then try to answer the questions.

1. What is happening in
this part of the story?

2. What are Rapunzel's tears
doing to the prince's eyes in
this part of the story?

3. Look back through
the story. Can you
see what is different
about this picture
of the **wicked witch**
and Rapunzel's father?

Complete your collection ...

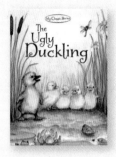

The Ugly Duckling

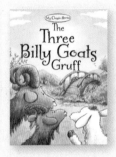

The Three Billy Goats Gruff

Hansel and Gretel

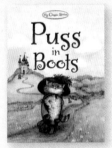

Puss in Boots

Little Red Riding Hood

Jack and the Beanstalk

Cinderella

The Gingerbread Man

The Emperor's New Clothes

Goldilocks and the Three Bears

Rapunzel

The Three Little Pigs

"Which one will you read next?"